This Book Belongs To:

....

Illustrated by Caroline Pedlar
Retold by Gaby Goldsack

This is a Parragon book
This edition published in 2006

Parragon
Queen Street House
4 Queen Street
Bath BA1 1HE, UK

Copyright © Parragon Books Ltd 2003

ISBN 1-40548-299-0
Printed in China

A Christmas Carol

p

One Christmas Eve, in old London town,
Ebenezer Scrooge looked out with a frown.
"Merry Christmas, Uncle!" called his cheery nephew.
"Come join in our festive dinner, won't you?"
"Bah, humbug!" growled Scrooge, "to Christmas Day!
What's merry about it? Now just go away!"

Poor Cratchit, his clerk, who worked hard each day,
asked Scrooge, "Is tomorrow a holiday?"
"I suppose you will want me to pay you as well!"
grumbled Scrooge who was mean, as I'm sure you can tell.
Scrooge hated Christmas because he was greedy.
He felt no pity for the poor and the needy.

Later that evening, when Scrooge was alone,
he heard rattling chains and a ghostly moan.
Then Scrooge saw poor Marley, who in happier days
was Scrooge's partner with the same selfish ways.
"Scrooge," wailed the ghost, "I've come to warn thee,
mend your mean ways, or you'll end up like me.

"Deep in the night, before Christmas Day,
three Spirits will come to show you the way."
With that, Marley's ghost then started to fade,
leaving Ebenezer Scrooge alone and afraid.
Scrooge was dismayed as he crept into bed.
But he drifted to sleep, despite his great dread.

As the clock struck one on that freezing night,
Ebenezer Scrooge awoke with a fright.
And as he blinked his eyes in the gloom,
an unearthly Spirit appeared in the room.
"Follow me," it said, as Scrooge looked aghast.
"I am the Ghost of Christmas Past!"

The ghost took Scrooge back to Christmases of old,
when Scrooge was warm-hearted, not sad and cold.
They saw Fan, his sister, and Fezziwig his boss.
"I was happy," gasped Scrooge, "not lonely and cross."
And as Scrooge was shown each old Christmas day,
he cried, "I can't bear it! Take me away!"

In the blink of an eye, Scrooge returned to his bed,
and was met by a jolly spirit who said,
"I am the good Ghost of Christmas Present.
Follow me now to see something pleasant."
In a flash, they were in Bob Cratchit's place,
which looked very festive, despite the cramped space.

Scrooge watched the Cratchits sit down to eat
their small Christmas dinner as if a great treat.
"God Bless us, every one," Tiny Tim cried,
as his family blessed him, smiling with pride.
"Tiny Tim," said the Spirit, "will always be lame.
But he is still cheerful, despite his great pain."

As the Spirit departed, another took shape –
a horrible creature in a hood and a cape.
It spoke not a word and seemed to be dumb.
It was the Ghost of Christmas Yet to Come.
At the graveyard it showed Scrooge what lay ahead:
misery and sorrow, for Tiny Tim was dead.

Then Scrooge saw his own grave, unloved and unkept,
alone in a cemetery where nobody wept.
As they wandered the streets, he heard people say,
"The old miser's gone, but who cares anyway?"
As the ghost disappeared Scrooge did something strange:
he fell down and wept, "Now I know I must change!"

The very next moment, Scrooge woke in his bed.
He raced to the window, then joyfully said,
"I haven't missed Christmas – what wonderful fun.
Merry Christmas," he called out, "to everyone!"
Then he stopped a small boy and asked humbly,
"Please take this turkey to the Cratchit family."

Then, handing out gifts, he tramped through the chill,
to call on his nephew and wish him goodwill.
And so began a most wonderful day,
full of laughter and joy, feasting and play.
Scrooge had been taught, as we hoped he would,
not to be mean, but giving and good!